Rickshaw Girl

O9-AIC-775

Rickshaw Girl

Mitali Perkins

Illustrated by

Jamie Hogan

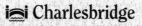 Charlesbridge

For Rob, with love—M. P.

For Daisy and Nirmala and precious daughters
everywhere—J. H.

2008 First paperback edition
Text copyright © 2007 by Mitali Perkins
Illustrations copyright © 2007 by Jamie Hogan
All rights reserved, including the right of reproduction in whole or in part in any
form. Charlesbridge and colophon are registered trademarks of Charlesbridge
Publishing, Inc.

Published by Charlesbridge
85 Main Street
Watertown, MA 02472
(617) 926-0329
www.charlesbridge.com

Library of Congress Cataloging-in-Publication Data
Perkins, Mitali.
    Rickshaw girl / Mitali Perkins ; illustrated by Jamie Hogan.
        p. cm.
    Summary: In her Bangladesh village, ten-year-old Naima excels at painting designs
called alpanas, but to help her impoverished family financially she would have to be
a boy—or disguise herself as one.
    ISBN 978-1-58089-308-4 (reinforced for library use)
    ISBN 978-1-58089-309-1 (softcover)
    [1. Painting—Fiction. 2. Sex role—Fiction. 3. Rickshaws—Fiction. 4. Family life—
Bangladesh—Fiction. 5. Bangladesh—Fiction.] I. Hogan, Jamie, ill. II. Title.
PZ7.P4315Ric 2007
[Fic]—dc22   2006009031

Printed in the United States of America
(hc) 10 9 8 7 6 5 4 3 2
(sc) 10 9 8 7 6 5 4 3

Illustrations done in pastels on Canson paper
Display type set in Marigold and text type set in Sabon
Color separations by Chroma Graphics, Singapore
Printed and bound by Lake Book Manufacturing, Inc.
Production supervision by Brian G. Walker
Designed by Susan Mallory Sherman

Rickshaw Girl

One

NAIMA RACED THROUGH her morning chores, trying hard to be careful. She washed the laundry in the river, making sure she didn't break any buttons this time. The other girls lazily sloshed clothes around, giggling and gossiping, but today Naima didn't stop to chat. She pumped four pails of water at the well, just as Mother had asked, and hauled them back one by one. She sliced eggplant, chili peppers, and onions in tiny, even cubes the way Mother liked them, instead of chopping them quickly into thick chunks the way she usually did.

"I've already wiped four banana leaf plates," Naima announced.

"Without tearing them?" Mother asked, her eyebrows rising like crows' wings.

"Not a rip in sight."

Mother smiled. "Well done, Naima. You may wait outside for Father."

Naima went quickly to the flat, wide stone just outside the doorway of their hut. Most of the homes in the village looked the same, with smooth clay walls, thatched roofs, dirt paths, and large stone thresholds. They only looked different on holidays, when girls decorated their family's paths and thresholds with painted patterns called *alpanas,* just as their ancestors had done for generations. In Naima's village, on International Mother Language Day, when the whole country celebrated the beauty of their Bangla language, the leaders gave a prize to the girl who painted the best *alpanas.*

Humming under her breath Naima carefully mixed up a batch of rice-powder paint. She'd invented a new pattern of curves, lines, and squares in her mind while doing her chores. Before she started painting she had to wipe off her last practice design. "Stop and *think* before you act," Mother often reminded her. But she never needed to warn Naima to be thoughtful when it came to painting *alpanas*.

Naima's sister Rashida came home from school. She started combing out her rag doll's hair and watched Naima erase the stone. "You're going to win again this year, Sister," she said.

"I hope so," Naima said. "We need another box of paints."

"And a new pad of paper," Rashida added.

Naima had made the prize last for months. She'd mixed colors from the paint box to create new ones. She and Rashida had discussed how to use each precious piece of fresh paper. Should Naima paint a crocodile slinking through lily pads? Or a monkey clutching a coconut as it swung from branch to branch? They picked the best paintings to brighten the dark clay walls inside their one-room hut.

The ring of a rickshaw bell made Naima look up. Saleem, their next-door neighbor, was pulling a passenger in his father's rickshaw. Naima watched his skinny legs turn the pedals as he puffed up the hill. The cycle was attached to a brightly painted tin cart with a leather bench and a decorated canopy that shaded customers from the sun.

"Why don't you and Saleem play together any more, Sister?" Rashida asked.

Naima dabbed her brush into the paint. She started a border of small circles that would go all the way around the big stone rectangle. "When you get older, Mother and the aunts will tell you not to talk to boys, too. They'll say it's not proper."

"I like playing with everybody at school," Rashida said. "Girls *and* boys."

You'll probably stop going soon anyway, Naima thought. Only Saleem knew how much she'd wanted to keep going to school. But Naima knew her parents couldn't afford to pay fees for two girls. Naima had studied for three years. Now it was Rashida's turn.

"You have to do more chores when you're ten," she said, sighing. "Saleem and I are both too busy to play these days."

Naima didn't tell her sister about the signal she and Saleem used when they wanted to meet. Saleem tucked a white handkerchief into his pocket. Naima tied a white bow on her braid. Once they'd finished their chores and eaten lunch in their own homes, they'd slip away to talk or play cards together behind the leafy banana trees. These days they only risked the signal for important meetings.

"You are getting old, Sister," Rashida said. "You probably won't be able to wear a *salwar kameez* much longer." Both sisters were dressed in cotton pants under long-sleeved tunics that came to their knees.

Naima made a face. "I know," she said. "And I can't move fast in a *saree*. Yards and yards of cloth that you have to wrap around yourself! They look pretty, but I feel as if I'm wearing a big bandage."

"Mother moves fast in her *saree*," Rashida said.

Naima knew her sister was trying to comfort her. "I suppose I will, too, once I get used to wearing one every day."

"I think it's hard to grow up," Rashida said, holding her rag doll close.

Naima didn't answer, but sometimes she felt the same way.

Two

FATHER WAS COMING DOWNHILL. The wheels of his rickshaw stirred up a flurry of dust. He raised a hand to greet the men who were playing cards in the shade of a mango tree. Their rickshaws all waited idly in the lane, and Father had to steer through a tangle of tin and tires. He parked in front of the hut.

Naima looked up from her *alpanas* to admire Father's gleaming new rickshaw. The tassels dangling from the handlebars were still swaying. The side panels were adorned with painted peacock feathers, green and gold and purple, the same color as the tassels. The bright blue of the lake that was painted on the rear panel matched the blue leather seat. White lotus flowers floated on the lake.

It was Rashida's turn to greet Father with a pail of river water. Father washed his face and hands, and gave her a kiss. "The marigolds need water, too, little one. They look as thirsty as I am."

Rashida headed for the small patch of flowers behind the hut. She leaned away from the heavy pail to keep her balance.

Naima was glad she'd pumped plenty of fresh drinking water from the well. Father could drink as much as he wanted inside the hut. He'd been out since dawn, hauling people and packages from place to place. Right after lunch he would head out again until midnight. She wished he could rest inside the cool clay hut. He needed to stay out of the hot sun like everybody else. But they had borrowed a lot of money to buy the rickshaw. If they didn't pay it back soon, they might lose the rickshaw. And then how would Father earn money?

"Your *alpanas* get better every day, Daughter," Father said, studying the design she was creating on the threshold.

"This one is not even halfway done yet," Naima answered. "I've only just started."

"Really? It looks so good already!"

"I'm going to paint a star in the middle," Naima told him.

Father stepped over the threshold. He turned to take one last look at the rickshaw before going inside. "Will you clean it for me, Naima?" he asked. "Nobody gets it as bright as you do."

"Of course, Father," Naima said. The unfinished *alpana* on the stone called out to her, but she jumped up and found a wet rag.

Even though she rushed through her other chores, Naima took her time cleaning Father's rickshaw. Rich people sometimes paid extra money to ride in a clean rickshaw. After scrubbing away most of the grime, she put the rag over one finger, held it in place with the other hand, and traced the outlines of the paintings. She polished the lotus flowers until they gleamed like ivory. The blue tin lake sparkled in the midday sunshine. Father's rickshaw was so new that these decorations were the original ones. Each time Naima cleaned the rickshaw, she imagined scenes the rickshaw painter might invent once these panels faded. Maybe a waterfall cascading down the snowy Himalayan mountains. Or a tiger, eyes blazing, peering through a leafy jungle.

Mother's worried voice drifted through the open door: "How much did you earn this morning, Husband?"

Naima tried not to listen, but she couldn't help it. She was glad Rashida was stooping over the marigolds in the back, too far away to hear.

"Not enough," Father replied.

Mother's sigh sounded like air leaking from a tire. Naima counted to five. She braced herself for words she'd overheard before. "If only *one* of our girls had been a boy!" Mother said.

Father gave his usual quick answer. "I have two wonderful daughters. They're just as good as boys."

"But you look so tired! Saleem takes his father's rickshaw out every afternoon so his father can rest. Our girls can't do that for you."

"Isn't Naima the best *alpana* painter in the village?" Father asked. "Doesn't she take care of her sister like a tiger guarding a cub? And Rashida is the best student in school!"

"Yes, but *alpanas* can't put rice on the table. And what use is it if Rashida is smart? We can't afford her school fees next year unless we pay off that rickshaw loan."

Rashida was coming back. Naima dunked the rag in the half-empty pail of water her sister was carrying. Fiercely, she scrubbed out her *alpana* design until no traces of the rice powder remained on the threshold.

"What are you doing, Sister?" Rashida asked. "You weren't finished! That was the best one yet!"

Naima didn't answer. Mother was right. All that a girl could do was cook, clean, wash clothes, and decorate; she wasn't allowed to do any work that brought in money. Painting *alpanas* wouldn't help Father get rest. Or add to their earnings. It was a waste of time.

"Rash-ee-da! Na-ee-ma! Come inside! Your father is hungry."

Saleem drove by again. This time a plump passenger sat on the bench of the rickshaw. He was a rich-looking passenger, juicy with money. Naima scowled and followed her sister into the hut.

Three

THE EGGPLANT CURRY and lentils were tasty, but Naima couldn't eat. Father *did* look tired. What if he got sick again? Last time he had coughed and shivered so badly that he hadn't been able to drive the rickshaw for weeks. They had used most of their savings to buy medicine.

If Father stayed healthy Naima was sure he would earn enough to provide food and pay back the rickshaw loan. But they could never afford the list of extras that she kept tucked inside her mind. A good supply of new paints and paper weren't the only items on the list. Mother wore that same faded cotton *saree* every day—she needed a new one made of silk to wear on holidays. Father didn't have a woolen shawl to keep him warm on cold nights. And Rashida glanced sadly into the sweet shop when the sisters passed it—she loved juicy *roshogollah* treats so much.

Naima spooned her lentils onto her sister's banana leaf. *If only I HAD been born a boy,* she thought. *Then I could earn some money. Even just a little would help!*

"Lie down for a few minutes, Husband," Mother urged. "You get so little rest. Even on Fridays you drive other men to the mosque before joining them to worship."

Father hesitated. He yawned. "Promise to wake me after fifteen minutes?"

"Of course," Mother said. She dimmed the window with an old sheet.

Slowly Father lowered himself onto the mat. He searched the darkened hut to find Naima. "Why don't you finish your *alpana* design, my daughter? That way you can keep an eye on the rickshaw, too."

"Yes, Father," Naima said, as she watched him slip almost instantly into sleep.

"Shh, girls," Mother said, tiptoeing around Father's quiet body. "Rashida, wipe off the plates. Didn't you hear your father, Naima? Go out and take care of that rickshaw!"

Naima went outside into the stifling noontime heat. The card-playing men had gone inside. Somewhere a radio was blaring Bangladesh's national anthem. Naima didn't feel like painting *alpanas*. Instead, still frowning, she climbed onto the leather bench of Father's rickshaw where the canopy provided some shade.

Saleem drove by again, this time with no passenger behind him. He glanced quickly around. Nobody was in sight, so he jumped off the cycle seat and walked over to Naima. "What's wrong?" he asked her.

Naima climbed down to join him. "You help *your* father," she burst out. "Why can't I help mine?"

Saleem shrugged. "You're a girl. Girls stay home and help their mothers. Boys earn money and work with their fathers. That's just the way it is."

"But why? It's not like that everywhere, Saleem. When I passed the tea stall this morning and peeked in at the television, I saw a Bangladeshi lady on the screen who was a *doctor.* And the last time he went to the city, Father told us he visited a shoe stand that was *owned* by a woman. If those women can do it, why can't I?"

"What are you going to do? Open a shoe stand here?"

Naima sighed. "That's the problem. I'd need money to do something like that. Besides, have you ever seen a girl—or even a woman—selling *anything* in our marketplace?"

"You're right," Saleem said. "I haven't."

They were quiet. Then: "Too bad I can't turn myself into a boy," Naima said.

"Yes! That would be great! We could play like

we used to—out in the open. You could join in our cricket games, and—Naima? Naima! Are you listening?"

Four

THE WHEELS IN NAIMA'S MIND were spinning wildly. She stared at Saleem's clothes. He wore a short *lungi,* a *kurta* shirt, and a cap. A cap that was just big enough to hide a girl's coiled braid.

"She's getting another one of her ideas," Saleem told his reflection in the rickshaw's tin panel. "Naima. Na-ee-ma! What are you thinking?"

"What if I *disguised* myself as a boy?" Naima asked. "I could drive Father's rickshaw for an hour or two every day. He'd have a chance to rest, and I could earn some money."

Saleem shook his head. "People will still recognize you."

"It might work at twilight," Naima said. "You can't see faces clearly at that time of day."

"Naima, it won't work, I tell you. Your passengers will know you're a girl as soon as they hear your voice."

"I wouldn't have to say much. Besides, I can sound like a boy. Listen to this." Naima deepened her voice: "Three *taka* for a ride to the marketplace and back."

Saleem grinned. "You sound more like a boy than I do," he said. "But this might be a good time to remember some history, Naima. Like the time you wanted us to walk all the way to the Dhaka zoo, for example. Even though it takes four hours to get there by train."

"We were only six years old. Father found us before it got dark."

"What about the time you almost drowned trying to catch fish with that new kind of net you invented?"

"I really thought those knots wouldn't break," Naima said, shrugging, "but they did. Anyway, you pulled me to shore in plenty of time. But this is different, Saleem. I'm older now. I'll ask Mother and Father for permission first."

"Even if they let you try wearing a disguise, which I'm sure they won't, somebody in the village will find out. They'll start gossiping. You'll bring shame to your whole family, Naima, and you don't want to do that."

"I don't care!" Naima said fiercely. "It's more shameful that I can't help by earning a little money. Besides, Mother and Father can keep a secret. Even Rashida knows how to hold her tongue. I'd promise to stay away from the relatives' huts."

Somebody switched off the radio, and Saleem climbed back on his cycle seat. "There has to be another way for you to earn some money," he told her. "We'll think of something, Naima."

"There *isn't* another way," Naima said, folding her arms and jutting out her chin.

Saleem sighed, shook his head, and drove away.

Naima stuck out her tongue at his back. *Easy for you to say,* she thought. *You're a boy.* She turned back to the rickshaw, and in her imagination she moved forward with her plan. First she'd convince her parents: "Father, you need rest. You can't get sick again. Mother, it's only an hour a day. Nobody will recognize me."

"What a wonderful idea, Naima," Mother would say. "You're so thoughtful."

"See? I told you a daughter's just as good as a son," Father would add. "I knew she could do it."

But could she? She squinted at Father's rickshaw, sparkling in the sunshine after her cleaning. It was beautiful, but it looked so heavy! She'd never driven one before. She was about the same size as Saleem though, and *he* managed to turn the pedals. She'd just have to show Father how good she was. Then he'd be sure to let her try it.

Five

NAIMA GLANCED AROUND. The village was silent; the lane empty. Quickly she climbed up on the cycle seat. She had to stand to reach both pedals at the same time. Grasping the handles for balance, she pressed hard with her feet.

The rickshaw didn't budge.

Naima pushed against the pedals with all her might.

The rickshaw started rolling downhill.

She was doing it! She was driving the rickshaw!

As she turned the pedals, Naima pictured Father's smile as she handed him the *taka* she had earned. In her mind's eye Mother got teary as she unwrapped a silk *saree* that Naima had picked out. An imaginary Rashida giggled as she popped one *roshogollah* after another into her mouth, devouring the whole pot that Naima had brought home from the sweet shop.

Before she realized what was happening, the lane began to curve at the bottom of the slope. A thicket of bushes loomed ahead. They were coming closer and closer. Desperately Naima tried to turn the rickshaw, but she couldn't seem to change directions. She squeezed the hand brakes as hard as she could, but the rickshaw seemed to pick up speed instead of slowing down. She couldn't steer it. She couldn't stop it.

Just before the rickshaw careened into the bushes, Naima managed to jump off the cycle. She landed on her hands and knees in the dusty lane. CRASH! The rickshaw just kept hurtling through the thicket like a stampeding animal.

Naima stayed where she was and listened to the rasp of thorns clawing the tin. Her heart was beating like a tabla drum. When everything was still, she stood up and made herself look. The thorns had captured Father's gleaming new rickshaw, bushes closing around it like a trap. Naima groaned and turned away.

Rashida was standing at the curve of the lane, her mouth as round as an *alpana* circle. Naima gestured at her sister, combing the air with her palm down, and Rashida raced down the hill. The two sisters struggled to pull out the rickshaw, but it was too heavy for them.

"Get Father," Naima said finally.

She sat on a rock and waited, her head in her hands. What had she done? Why hadn't she stopped to think? Mother was right—Naima *was* too thoughtless. Saleem had been right, too—this had been another one of her silly ideas.

Father and Mother and Rashida came running. Mother gathered Naima close. Then she held her out at arm's length, scanning her face, hands, body. "Are you bleeding?" she asked.

"*I'm* all right, Mother, but—" Naima's voice broke.

Father was already in the bushes. Somehow he managed to wrestle the rickshaw back onto the lane. All four of them gasped when they saw the scratches on the leather and the dents on the tin. The peacock feathers on the side panels were torn and ragged. Even the painted lotus flowers on the back panel had been clawed by the thorns.

"Eesh!" Mother wailed. "You've ruined the rickshaw, Naima! What were you thinking?"

"I—I was trying to drive it."

"*What?* Why in the world would you do something like that?"

"I'm sorry," Naima managed to say, fighting back tears. "I was trying to see if I could drive it so—so that I could give Father a rest." It was too late to explain her whole idea. She knew they'd never let her try it now.

"The sun has been shining too hot on your head, Daughter!" Mother scolded. "Have you ever seen a girl driving a rickshaw? I thought you were growing up, Naima, but you're as careless as ever!"

Father didn't say anything. His face was grim. He climbed on and pushed the pedals. The rickshaw moved slowly, like an ox obeying its master even though it didn't want to.

"It still works," Father called over his shoulder, heading for the hut.

Naima could hear the relief in his voice. She spanked the dust off her hands and clothes, hard, and trudged uphill slowly behind Mother and Rashida.

Six

FATHER HAD PARKED the rickshaw in front of the hut. Naima kept her eyes down as she passed it. Inside she went straight to her mat and pulled the sheet over her head. She felt the thump of her sister landing cross-legged beside her. A small hand fumbled under the sheet to find hers.

"We need to repair it soon," Mother was saying. "With such a ruined rickshaw, you won't get any business for weddings or other parties."

"Both of the repair shops in our village are too expensive," Father said. "And they don't do good work."

"Where will you take it?"

"I heard a rumor that Hassan's Rickshaw Repair

Shop is opening up again in the next village. Old Hassan was the best rickshaw painter for miles around. 'The best work at the best prices,' he used to brag, and he was right. One of his sons must have decided to start the business up again. I'll take the rickshaw there as soon as it opens."

"It's going to be expensive," Mother said. "We'll have to get it painted again *and* fix the dents and tears."

"Let me see how much extra money I'll need to make." Naima heard the rattling sound of the tin bank they kept in the wardrobe.

"We can't use that money," Mother said. "That's for Rashida's school fees. Here, take this instead. We'll have to trade it for the repairs."

Naima yanked the sheet off her head. It was just as she'd feared. Mother had twisted off one of the two gold bangles she always wore on her wrist. She was holding it out to Father.

Naima saw Father looking deep into Mother's eyes. "You were wearing these on our wedding day," he said.

Mother smiled. "What's mine is yours, remember?"

Father took the bangle and put it back on Mother's wrist. Naima waited for him to declare that he'd never sell it. Instead he said, "We'll trade it only if I can't earn enough money."

Naima couldn't believe it. That bangle had been given to her great-grandmother by *her* mother. The soft clinking of two circles had always made music for their family. Now they might lose that music forever. She lay down and covered her face again with the sheet, wishing she didn't ever have to take it off. The tears were coming fast now. She heard the rustle of her sister getting up. She felt the weight of Father's palm on her covered head, resting there for a moment. His footsteps crossed the stone threshold. The bell of the rickshaw chimed as he drove away.

Someone gently pulled back the sheet. A soft hand smoothed the tangled hair off her forehead. A low voice began a familiar lullaby. Naima wiped her tears and drew a shaky breath. The pain inside her heart loosened a bit. The pair of bangles was still singing on Mother's wrist. Maybe Father *could* earn the money for the repairs.

Seven

AFTER THE CRASH Father no longer came home for lunch. He was trying to find passengers while other rickshaws sat idle. He stayed out until midnight in case somebody needed an emergency ride. But Mother had been right. People didn't like the look of such a battered and dented rickshaw. They didn't trust a driver who had let his rickshaw get into such a state.

Every afternoon Naima searched Father's face. The bangle was still on Mother's wrist, but for how long? How many days could he work from dawn until midnight without getting sick?

A couple of aunts came to visit, sitting outside on the threshold with Mother. "What's wrong with Naima?" one of them asked. "We heard she crashed your rickshaw. Why in the world was she driving it, anyway?"

Mother bristled. "Everybody makes mistakes. She was only trying to help. She's growing up, you know."

Mother came inside to make tea, and the voices outside became whispers that carried into the hut. "Wrecking a rickshaw is growing up? Doesn't sound like she was trying to help. Something must be wrong with that girl."

Saleem rode by, ringing his bell loudly, the white handkerchief poking out of his pocket. He even took it out and pretended to blow his nose, trying to make sure Naima spotted the signal. But she didn't push back the window covering and wave. She didn't dash outside so they could exchange a few words. And she certainly didn't slip over to the banana grove to meet him. *I'm already a disgrace*, she thought. *If my aunts catch me spending time with a boy, I'll bring even more shame to Mother.*

During the next couple of weeks, Saleem made

several more attempts before the handkerchief disappeared and he stopped ringing the rickshaw bell. Naima peeked at him from behind the curtain, fiddling with the white ribbon she kept hidden on her wrist under the long sleeve of her *salwar kameez*. Life was closing in around her like the bushes had closed in around the rickshaw. She even wished that her parents would punish her for what she had done. But after scolding her that first day, Mother never brought it up again. She seemed to think Naima was feeling bad enough.

"Our daughter's so sad these days," she told Father one night, when she thought the girls were asleep. "She doesn't rush through her chores to paint *alpanas*. She doesn't chatter nonstop about crazy ideas and plans. She moves so slowly and keeps so quiet, I hardly know she's there."

"She'll be herself again soon," Father said. "As soon as we get that rickshaw fixed."

Father's confidence helped a little, but Naima still felt empty and numb. When she closed her eyes, the only thing she could picture was Father's beaten and bruised rickshaw. The image of it blocked the *alpana* designs that used to dazzle her mind with color. She could hardly remember the countless ideas that used to spin in her mind as she washed clothes or chopped vegetables.

International Mother Language Day, February 21st, came and went. Naima couldn't bring herself to decorate the family's hut even though Rashida pleaded with her to try. Rashida and Mother did their best, but the prize went to a girl on the other side of the village.

Relatives gathered at a great-uncle's house to eat *biryani* chicken and celebrate the holiday. Naima's aunts wore new silk *sarees,* rustling like wind in the rice paddies. Mother put on her party *saree,* the one she wore every year. Naima noticed the patch she was trying to hide, and how faded the *saree* looked among the bright colors of the others.

"Any news about the repair shop in the next village?" Father asked.

"I think it's opening next week," someone answered. "Hassan's prices and work were always the best for miles around. The crooks who run the shops around here are spreading rumors about that shop already."

"What are they saying?"

"Oh, I don't believe anything they say. They

don't want to lose our business, so they're making up all kinds of crazy stories."

"They're probably telling the truth," an older uncle said. "The old man tried to train his sons, but neither one was as good as he was."

"I'll let you know what I find out," Father promised.

After the holiday the days slipped back into their pattern. Rashida was back at school. Father was working day and night. Mother and Naima were doing the household chores in silence. And Saleem was riding by stony-faced, keeping his eyes straight ahead as he steered his father's rickshaw up and down the lane.

Eight

ONE DAY FATHER surprised them by coming home early for lunch. "The rickshaw's looking worse than ever," he said. "It's starting to rust. And Hassan's shop should be open for business by now. I'll go there today, and if it's open, I'll price the repairs."

"But . . . have you earned enough money, Father?" Naima asked, even though she knew the answer.

The hut was quiet. Slowly Mother eased a bangle over her hand and handed it to Father. He slipped the bangle inside his pocket and fastened the button Mother had sewn on his shirt to keep his earnings safe.

Naima's stomach clenched like a fist. She wanted to shout, cry, rip the pocket open and grab the bracelet, but she knew it was no use. Mother's graceful movements would never make music again. And it was all Naima's fault.

Father cleared his throat. "I'll earn enough money to buy another bangle soon."

The four of them ate rice and spinach and lentils in silence. Naima made herself chew and swallow, longing to fling herself on her mat and cover her face. But after lunch Father took her hand and led her out into the bright, hot light.

"Look at our *alpanas,* Naima."

"I did already, Father."

"Look closely."

Naima let her eyes dwell on the fading patterns that Mother and Rashida had hastily invented for the contest. She stifled a groan. She hadn't cared much on International Mother Language Day, but now the mistakes made her feel even worse.

"Do you think you can improve our *alpanas?*" Father asked.

"The contest's over, Father," Naima said.

"What's the use of fixing them now? We lost the prize."

"Don't do it for the prize," Father said. "Make them right for *their* sake." He dropped a kiss on her head and climbed on the cycle seat. "Tell Mother not to wait up. I'll head to the repair shop once the customers get scarce."

Naima watched him pull away in the beat-up rickshaw, her heart sinking. Mother's bangle would be gone by the time he got home. She turned to frown once more at the *alpanas* on the threshold. The patterns were so . . . off-balance. If they'd added a square in this corner and one more paisley on the other two, the weight of the whole design would have worked better.

Rashida was standing at the door. Silently she handed her sister the leftover white rice-powder paste, the brushes, the colored paints made from burnt earth, lentils, and spices. Then she turned and disappeared.

Before Naima could stop herself, her mind began to dance with colors, shapes, sizes, balance, symmetry, patterns. Soon her hands were flying to keep up. She painted for a while, humming under her breath, forgetting everything but her work. Then she sat back and took stock of what she had done.

The revised alpanas on the step didn't look like the design she might have invented if she'd started from scratch. Those would have been good. But as she looked closely, Naima had to admit the truth, even to herself: these might actually be *better*.

Nine

THE IDEA CAME WHEELING into her mind as though it had been waiting for the chance. She was still the best *alpana* painter in the village, wasn't she? Surely painting rickshaws wasn't much harder than designing *alpanas*. Why couldn't she work for the rickshaw painter in exchange for the rickshaw repair?

Think this through, Naima, she warned herself sternly.

Men in the village sometimes traded work with each other. Saleem had burned garbage the week before in exchange for roof repairs on his family's hut. The rickshaw repair shops in Naima's village always hired a boy or two as helpers.

Naima pulled the white ribbon from under the sleeve of her *salwar kameez*. After tying it in a bow around her braid, she swung the braid in front of her shoulder and waited for Saleem to drive by. She saw his eyes widen as he picked up her signal. Making sure Mother and Rashida were still asleep, she slipped away to meet him.

The banana leaves stirred up a breeze as Saleem pushed through them. "Naima! I was so glad to see that ribbon again. Why have you been avoiding me?"

For the first time in her life, Naima couldn't meet his eyes. "I—I—er . . . "

"Are we still friends?" Saleem asked.

Naima looked up and saw the familiar nut-brown face, the dark eyebrows that met in the middle of Saleem's forehead, the almond eyes full of concern. "We'll always be friends," she said.

Saleem's teeth gleamed like the inside of a coconut. "So what's your new plan?" he asked.

"How'd you know I have a plan?"

He shrugged. "I've known you ever since you were born, Naima. Some of your ideas are crazy, but you always think of something. And a few of them are really good."

"They are? Like what?"

"You invented that new color for *alpanas* by mixing crushed marigold petals with papaya rinds, remember? That's one reason you won the prize last year. And you came up with our secret signal, too. Which nobody's figured out yet."

Naima smiled for what felt like the first time in a long while. Saleem was right: some of her ideas did work.

"So what have you come up with this time?" he asked.

He looked doubtful as he listened to her explanation. "You'll be in heaps of trouble when your parents find out," he said. "They'll never let you go to the shop again. How are you going to earn enough to pay for the repairs?"

"I have the rest of this afternoon and all evening to paint, don't I? I can pay for a small part of the repairs at least. When Father arrives, I'll just show him my work. There's a chance he might let me go back and earn the rest, Saleem. He wants to save Mother's bangle as much as I do."

"But you've never painted rickshaws before, Naima. *Alpanas* are different."

Naima was silent. A part of her mind had been wondering the same thing ever since she came up with the plan. *Could* she paint a rickshaw?

Saleem stood up suddenly. "You should give it a try. Sitting around doing nothing is harder for you than making mistakes and getting in trouble. I'll help you do this, Naima." Before she could say anything, he ran out of the banana grove.

She couldn't believe how quickly he returned, carrying a bundle under his arm.

"Nobody's awake yet," he said. "But you'll need to hurry. And be careful."

"Our villages are safe," Naima said. "I'll be fine."

"You'll be a stranger there, and it's about an hour's walk away. I wish I could drive you, but I have to get some paying fares. Father's going to wonder already what I've been doing all afternoon."

Naima tugged the white ribbon off her braid. "Here—this is for you."

"For me? Why?"

"It's a present, a keepsake, to remember that we're friends, even if we can't meet here as often as we used to. Now you leave first, and I'll come out after a few minutes."

As she walked back to the hut, Saleem drove by. He rang the bell and waved, making sure she saw the strip of white gleaming around his wrist.

The single room of the hut was dim and hushed. Mother and Rashida's sleeping bodies hadn't moved. Naima knew that they wouldn't start to worry until it got dark. Mother sometimes allowed Naima to visit a cousin on the other side of the village, and Naima had forgotten to ask for permission once or twice before heading out. She was counting on Mother thinking that she'd forgotten again.

She opened the bundle Saleem had handed her. Inside, she found a cap, a *lungi* cloth, and a *kurta* shirt. They were the fancy set that he wore to the mosque. Silently she took off her *salwar kameez* and put on the boy's clothes, tucking her braid carefully under the cap.

Ten

THE VILLAGE WAS SLOWLY waking up. It wouldn't be long before the lanes were bustling with rickshaws and people. The tea stall owner was boiling a big kettle of water. His television, the only one in the neighborhood, would draw a big crowd of men who wanted to watch the afternoon news and drink tea. Other vendors along the street were starting to arrange their wares—rubber sandals, wool shawls, toys, baskets of pomegranates, cinnamon sticks, and cloves.

At first Naima felt odd in Saleem's clothes. She kept away from other people, worried that they'd see through her disguise. As the streets began to fill, though, an older boy walking in the opposite direction came quite close, looked right at her, and then peered over her shoulder to catch a glimpse of someone else. Other villagers who were starting to stir up the lanes with noise and dust didn't seem to notice anything unusual about Naima either.

Only a few women and girls her age were out walking. They stood out like marigold blossoms in the grass. Everybody stared at them. Naima strode along in her disguise, enjoying the freedom from curious eyes. *How easy to be a boy,* she thought. *I could go into the tea stall and watch television if I wanted. I could stop and bargain with fruit sellers.* But she didn't have time to linger. She had to get to that repair shop before Father did! She forced herself not to think about Father's reaction when he found her.

After leaving the marketplace Naima took a shortcut, splashing through rice paddies. She found the lane that led to the other village and trotted along it. She knew the way; Father had taken her and Rashida there for a drive after bringing the new rickshaw home. What she didn't know was how to find the new repair shop.

A boy about her age was selling bananas in the center of the other village. "Three *taka* a dozen!" he was shouting.

Naima strode up to him, confident now in her disguise. "Do you know where the new rickshaw repair shop is?" she asked, remembering to deepen her voice.

"By the pond," the boy said, steadying his basket as he tipped his chin to show her the direction. "Why do you want to go there?"

"I'm hoping the new owner might need a helper. Do you know if the shop's hired someone already?"

The boy smirked. "Not that I know of," he said. "You'd have to be desperate to want that job."

Naima could tell he was hoping she'd ask more questions, but she didn't have time for gossip. "I *am* desperate," she said, forgetting to lower her voice. She headed in the direction of the shop, leaving him staring after her.

The shadows of the coconut trees were growing tall and thin when Naima reached the pond. She spotted the shop immediately—a small hut in a yard littered with rickshaw panels, tools, cans of paint, leather benches, and tires. She glimpsed an older woman standing beside a stack of tin panels. Naima knew she was a widow because only women who had lost their husbands wore white *sarees*.

"Excuse me," Naima said politely, coming up behind the woman. "Is this Hassan's Rickshaw Repair Shop?" This time she remembered to lower her voice.

"What do you want? Can't you see that I'm busy?"

Did everybody have to waste precious time by asking questions? Naima fought to make her voice sound patient and respectful. "My father's rickshaw needs repairs," she answered. "I came to see if I could do some work in exchange for them. May I see the repairman to ask him this favor?"

"I *am* the repairman," the woman said.

Eleven

NAIMA'S HEAD WHIRLED and her mouth fell open. This widow was the owner of a rickshaw repair shop? Here—in a village just like her own? How could that be? But the woman had half-turned to see her, and that was a brush in her hand. That was paint staining her *saree*. Naima hadn't noticed the shining rectangle of unpainted tin propped up in front of her.

"My first order, and only one day to complete it," the woman was saying, almost as if she were talking to herself. "I need to concentrate, and all I get are interruptions." She didn't bother keeping the irritation out of her voice.

Naima didn't move. The woman made an

exasperated noise and went back to work. Naima peered over her shoulder as the woman dipped the brush in a pot of yellow paint. The slim, stained fingers guided the brush, leaving a trail of yellow leaves across the tin.

"I could help you," Naima said suddenly. "I paint the best *alpanas* in my village."

The woman sighed but didn't stop painting. "Are you still here?" she asked. "Why don't you go and bother someone else? We both know that boys don't paint *alpanas*."

Naima took off her cap and let her braid tumble down. "I'm not a boy," she said.

The woman's brush stopped in midair. She placed the brush in a jar of water and turned around again. All the way, this time. "A-re!" she said, looking as amazed as Naima must have when Naima had discovered her identity. "Why are you dressing up like that, then?"

The story poured out of Naima like water from a pitcher. ". . . and it was all my fault," she ended. "I can't earn money because I'm a girl, so I borrowed these clothes."

"Who says girls can't earn money?" the woman asked. She adjusted her *saree*, folded her arms across her chest, and jutted out her chin.

Something about the woman's stance seemed familiar, but Naima didn't stop to figure out what it was. "I don't know who made the rule," she answered. "But it's always been like that."

"Things are changing whether people around here like it or not. These days a woman who wants to start her own business can borrow money from our women's bank. We decided to put our money together and help each other."

"Is that what you did? Borrow money from the women's bank?"

The woman nodded. "After my husband died all I had left were these." She made her ten fingers bow and straighten in front of Naima's eyes. "Thankfully, while my father was teaching my brothers the trade, I always tagged along and learned everything I could. Neither of my brothers wanted to run the shop, so Father closed it down before he died. He had no idea *I'd* be the one to open it up again."

"Are you making money?" Naima asked eagerly, not bothering to wonder if the question was rude. It felt like the most important question in the world.

The woman didn't seem to mind. "I've only

been open for a few days. This order's for my cousin Ali's rickshaw fleet. If he likes my work, he's promised to give me more business—*and* spread the word. People have always followed Ali's lead."

As she listened Naima caught sight of an old-fashioned rickshaw. It was freshly painted with borders of orchids and lilies and water hyacinths outlining each panel. The words "Hassan's Rickshaw Repair Shop" were emblazoned on the back panel. And each of the side panels declared: "The best work at the best prices." The painter had used bright yellow paint to form the perfect Bangla lettering. Something about the borders that decorated each panel reminded Naima of an *alpana* design.

Meanwhile the rickshaw woman was studying Naima's hands. "Hmm," she said thoughtfully. "I *could* use some help—Ali won't give me more business if I don't finish by tomorrow, even if he is family. Painting a rickshaw panel from scratch requires a lot of training, but I might let you try touching up one of the panels that still looks somewhat decent." She moved her fingers quickly down the stack, stopping to tap a corner of tin about halfway up from the ground. "Take this panel and let me see what you do with it. It won't take me much time to fix if you make too many mistakes. But watch me for a while before you start. Applying enamel paint on tin is quite different than painting rice powder on a stone."

The sun was sinking low and the evening call to prayer from the village mosque echoed across the pond. Mother was going to start worrying soon, but Naima couldn't leave now. The woman lit a few kerosene lanterns and went back to her painting. Naima watched the woman closely, noticing how much paint she placed on the brush and the way it was supposed to be held in the hand.

After a while Naima gathered her courage. She carefully moved a half-dozen panels one by one, making a new stack beside the first one until she uncovered the faded one the woman had tapped. Placing it on the ground by itself, she squinted at the painting. A border of marigolds edged their way around the whole rectangle. They framed two white doves perched on a rock beside a pond. Close by, a tiger was bending his head to drink.

Taking a deep breath Naima squatted in front of the panel. She chose a clean brush and dipped it into the pot of orange. She gripped the brush firmly, just as the woman did, and started painting. It wasn't hard to follow the original painter's lines. After finishing the flowers, she cleaned the doves' dirty feathers with a coat of fresh white enamel. She brightened the yellow stripes on the tiger's fur. With a wider brush she splashed blue across the pond, making it sparkle like the one on the back of Father's rickshaw.

"I'm finished," she called out when she was satisfied with the painting.

The woman came over, and Naima held her breath. Would her work be good enough? "There's a mistake here and there," the woman said, patting Naima's shoulder. "But it's actually quite good. I'll fix the mistakes later. Let's keep working, shall we? We just might complete this order if we both keep going."

Naima nodded her agreement. The woman chose another panel from the unfinished stack, and Naima started painting it. She smoothed the curves of petals. She straightened the tips of stars. She tidied the tails of fish. She washed the brush again and again.

"We did it!" the woman said finally, her voice jubilant. "Ali's going to be delighted!"

Naima had touched up four faded panels. The woman had fixed Naima's mistakes as well as completely cleaning, scraping, and repainting eight panels. Now the dozen panels were spread around the yard to dry. Pearly palaces, pink roses, purple birds, and golden rice paddies glowed softly in the light of the kerosene lamps.

Suddenly a rickshaw came riding out of the darkness. To Naima's amazement, Father jumped off the cycle and strode over to them. In her fierce concentration over her work, she'd forgotten that Father was supposed to come to the shop after his evening route. She'd even forgotten that she was still dressed like a boy. What would Father say when he recognized her?

"Have you seen a girl—" Father began. Then he caught sight of Naima. For a long minute he stared at her in the dim light, too stunned even to speak. Then: "*Naima!* You came here *alone?* Dressed like *that?* We've been frantic with worry. *What* were you thinking?"

For the first time ever, Naima heard anger ringing in Father's voice.

Twelve

"DON'T SCOLD HER," the woman said quickly. "She came here to work in exchange for the repairs on your rickshaw. She wanted to make things right. Not many people are brave enough to try that."

"Well, Naima?" Father asked sternly. "I asked you a question."

"I—I—" All she could think of was to echo the rickshaw woman's words. "I wanted to make things right, Father. Because of the rickshaw— that's why I came."

Father's gaze traveled around the dark yard. "Where is the rickshaw repairman? Why has he kept you here for so long?"

Naima moved closer to him. "*She's* the owner

of the shop, Father," she whispered, tipping her head in the direction of the woman.

Father was silent. Naima knew he was trying to make sense of what she had just told him. "I heard there was a new repair shop here," he said finally to the woman. "Is yours the only one?"

The woman nodded. "My father used to own a shop in this village. And my shop will live up to his motto—'The best work at the best prices.' See for yourself."

"Do, Father," Naima added softly. "Please."

"All right," Father said. The shock of discovering the woman's identity seemed to have completely erased his anger.

He walked around the yard slowly, studying the drying panels. The woman accompanied him, holding the kerosene lantern high. Naima waited nervously beside Father's rickshaw.

"Your work *is* good," Father said to the woman, when the two of them rejoined Naima. Naima caught the ring of truth in his voice.

"This isn't only my work," the woman said quickly. "Your daughter repainted those four panels. That's why I kept her here for so long. I wanted to see if she could do it."

"You did? She did? I'm not surprised, because she paints—"

"—the finest *alpanas* in the village. She told me. I don't doubt it. Now let me take a look at your rickshaw."

The woman fingered the dents and stroked the scratched panels as though the rickshaw were alive. "I can have it ready for you by tomorrow night," she said. "It will be as good as new—perhaps even better."

"How much will it cost?" Father asked, fumbling with the button that fastened the pocket on his shirt. Naima caught her breath.

"I won't take money," the woman said. "I'll charge you . . . the price of a promise."

"Excuse me?" Father's fingers came out again, empty. Naima started breathing again.

"Your daughter's just the right age to learn the trade," the woman said. "If you promise to bring her here three or four afternoons a week, I'll fix your rickshaw in exchange for her labor. And train her on top of it. If she's a good worker, and our business picks up, I might even start paying her."

Naima couldn't believe her ears. Could this be happening? Had the woman really said "*our* business"? But then she realized that Father was quiet. He was looking at Naima, almost as if he were asking her a question. Naima didn't say anything, but she let her longing to take this chance show on her face.

Father turned back to the woman. "What about your sons?" he asked. "Don't they want to be trained? They could run the shop for you one day."

"My daughters were married years ago. Both are busy with their own lives in faraway villages. I have no sons."

"Neither do I," said Father.

"But you *do* have a daughter with talent. And I'd like to train her to paint rickshaws."

Naima kept her eyes on Father. He'd always insisted that daughters were as good as sons. Now he had the chance to prove that he meant it. His hand traveled once more toward his pocket, but it stopped in midair, changed direction, and landed on Naima's shoulder instead. "I'm proud to make such a promise," he told the woman. "My daughter is a good girl. She learns quickly and will serve you well."

Naima's mind raced ahead to the long afternoon rests Father would take before driving her to the repair shop. A box of new paints, a butter-yellow silk *saree*, a gray woolen shawl, and a pot of juicy *roshogollah* paraded before her eyes. She wanted to leap and shout and do a victory dance around the battered rickshaw. She wanted to throw her arms around it and plant kisses on the leather, tin, and tassels. But instead she reached for Father's hand and felt his fingers tighten around hers.

Thirteen

"I'LL LET YOU BORROW my rickshaw until tomorrow evening," the woman said, pointing to the old-fashioned one decorated with advertisements for the shop. "It will be a good way for your village to know that Hassan's is back in business."

"Don't worry," said Father. "I'll tell everybody that you're as good as your father. He was an honest man and a talented painter."

The woman turned to Naima, smiling. "It's a good thing you turned out to be a girl with plenty of *alpana* experience. I don't think I'd have given a boy a chance."

The woman's rickshaw was ancient, but well

oiled. Father pedaled hard and they sped through the dark village. *It's a good thing I turned out to be a girl.* The words chimed like sitar music in Naima's mind.

"How did you know where I was, Father?" Naima asked.

Father slowed down and threw the words over his shoulder. "I finally tracked Saleem down. It took a while because he'd taken a passenger all the way to the hospital in town."

The rickshaw picked up speed again. The wind slapped against Naima's cheeks and blew her hair loose from her braid. She held tightly to Saleem's cap so she wouldn't lose it. They'd come up with their secret-keeping policy in the shade of the banana grove: "Tell only if one of us might be in trouble." She'd have to borrow Rashida's white ribbon to use as a signal; she couldn't wait to see Saleem's face when he heard her news.

Mother was awake when they got home. Her eyes widened at the sight of Naima in the borrowed *lungi* and *kurta* shirt but she didn't say anything. Instead she pulled Naima into her lap. She combed out Naima's tangled hair and re-braided it while Father told her the whole story.

"Who would have thought that a girl could be trained to work as a rickshaw painter?" Mother asked. "Times are certainly changing. Of course we'd never let Naima do this if the owner of the repair shop had been one of Hassan's sons. It's a good thing she turned out to be a daughter instead."

Just like me, Naima thought.

She stretched out on her mat beside her sleeping sister, tiredness making her aware of every muscle that she had used during the day. In the flickering lamplight Father gently twisted the golden bangle over Mother's outstretched hand. Once again, the tinkling melody of two bangles filled the hut. Naima smiled as she listened. Now the music that belonged to her family was going to last forever.

Glossary of Bangla Words

alpana: Girls and women paint these geometrical or floral patterns on the floor during celebrations and holidays. They use crushed rice powder to outline the design, and decorate with colored chalk, vermilion, flower petals, wheat, or lentil powder. Some designs are passed down from generation to generation for hundreds of years.

a-re: A Bangla exclamation that means something like "Hey!" or "What's going on around here?"

Bangla: The national language of Bangladesh. It's the official language of West Bengal, a state in India, and the fourth most widely spoken language in the world.

biryani: A slow-cooked, aromatic rice dish served on special occasions, usually mixed with lamb, chicken, or mutton. The savory fragrance comes from rose water, whole spices, and saffron.

eesh: Depending on the speaker's tone of voice, this Bangla exclamation means that something has happened that is shameful, disappointing, or disastrous.

International Mother Language Day: Also known as Ekushey February, this national holiday celebrated on February 21st commemorates the first martyrs killed in Bangladesh's struggle for independence from Pakistan. On February 21, 1952, police shot and killed several university students who were campaigning for the recognition of the Bangla language as one of the state languages of Pakistan. Bangladesh eventually gained independence from Pakistan in 1971.

kurta: Boys and men wear this knee-length shirt over drawstring trousers called pajamas, or over a *lungi*.

lungi: A man or boy wears this loop of cloth that hangs from the waist to the ankle, like a long skirt. He gathers the cloth in front at the waist, twists it into a half-knot, and tucks the ends in.

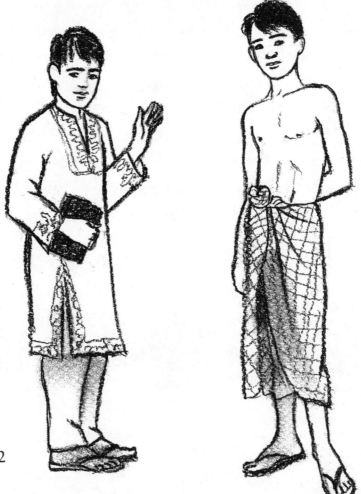

rickshaw: This is a vehicle that people hire for transportation. In Bangladesh, a person pedals a cycle attached to a seat carrying passengers.

roshogollah: These traditional Bengali treats are spongy balls of sweetened cottage cheese drenched in syrup.

salwar kameez: Girls wear this three-piece outfit that consists of a *kameez*, a long shirt or tunic, a *salwar*, or loose pajama-like trousers, and a *dupatta*, a long scarf or shawl.

saree: A long garment made of five to six yards of cloth that a woman wraps, pleats, and tucks around her waist and then drapes over her shoulder. It's usually worn over a tight-fitting blouse and a petticoat.

tabla: Two drums, one made of wood and a larger one made of metal, covered with goat or cow skin, and played with the fingers, palm, and heel of the hand.

taka: The official currency of Bangladesh. One dollar was equal to sixty-four *taka* at the time of this writing.

Author's Note

ASK SOMEONE on this side of the planet, "What do you know about the villages of Bangladesh?"

You might hear an answer like this: "They're desperately poor, densely populated, and often hit by cyclones and tidal waves."

Here's what you should tell them: "You'd be surprised. There are treasures to discover in rural Bangladesh. You'll stumble across jewels that aren't for sale—emerald rice paddies, golden jute fields, ruby sunsets in a sapphire sky. There are pleasures, too, that you can't buy—the hospitality and courtesy of village families, their artistic expressions of music, dance, drama, *alpana* painting, and rickshaw art. You'll be encouraged, because you'll see lives beginning to change, and families coming out of poverty for the first time in ages."

For countless generations my own ancestors lived and farmed jute in what is now Bangladesh. Although I was born in Kolkata, India, and raised in the United States, returning to rural Bangladesh felt strangely like a homecoming. During the three years that my husband and I lived in Dhaka, Bangladesh's capital city, we learned about the many ways international relief and development workers are trying to fight poverty. One of the most successful efforts is in the field of microfinance, spearheaded mainly by Bangladeshis.

What is microfinance? It's setting up a fund so that a person can borrow small amounts of money and invest it in a way that makes more money. A borrower can buy a goat, for example, and sell the milk. Or she can purchase a bicycle so that someone in her family can work as a delivery person. Once she starts earning money from the investment, she pays the loans back at a fair interest rate so that more people in the village are able to borrow money from the fund. Studies show that, in general, women are better than men at investing a loan in a way that benefits the whole family. That's why microfinance with a focus on women is a powerful weapon in the war against poverty.

Before the funds were set up, traditional banks weren't willing to risk a loan to someone who wasn't already making money, especially to women who didn't usually work outside of the home. A village woman's only option was to approach the local moneylender, who usually charged high rates of interest. Her situation then grew even more desperate as she tried to pay the money back. Now, because of microfinance, women like the painter in *Rickshaw Girl* are able to borrow money, set up businesses, and hire and train apprentices like Naima.

Girls in the villages of Bangladesh now have hope that they, too, can help their families, but there's still a long way to go. If you want to get involved, please write to me via my website (www.mitaliperkins.com), and I'll introduce you to good people on the frontlines who can use your help. I hope you enjoyed Naima's story.

Acknowledgments

The authenticity of the *alpanas* in this book was verified by Madhusree Bose, my mother, who beautified our California home with the art, cooking, fashion, music, dance, and embroidery of Bengal.

My father, Sailendra Nath Bose, told me countless tales of his boyhood in Faridpur, Bangladesh, and rejoiced in the gift of three daughters.

Alex Counts, president of the Grameen Foundation, USA, arranged a once-in-a-lifetime visit to my ancestral village and enlightened me about the power of microcredit.

Dr. Sajeda Amin of the Population Council

gave advice on the customs and dress of Muslim women and girls in Bangladeshi villages.

Editor Judy O'Malley shepherded Naima's story from start to finish, caring for it as diligently as she nurtures writers. Thanks also to Susan Sherman, art director, and artist Jamie Hogan for their visionary, magical partnership in creating this book.

Last but far from least, I'm grateful for the countless rickshaw drivers who safely and cheerfully transported my husband, Rob, me, and our babies through the streets of Dhaka.

image comics presents

ROBERT KIRKMAN
CREATOR, WRITER

CHARLIE ADLARD
PENCILER, INKER

CLIFF RATHBURN
GRAY TONES

RUS WOOTON
LETTERER

CHARLIE ADLARD
&
CLIFF RATHBURN
COVER

SINA GRACE
EDITOR

SKYBOUND™

For SKYBOUND ENTERTAINMENT

Robert Kirkman - CEO
J.J. Didde - President
Sina Grace - Editorial Director
Shawn Kirkham - Director of Business Development
Tim Daniel - Digital Content Manager
Chad Manion - Assistant to Mr. Grace
Sydney Pennington - Assistant to Mr. Kirkham
Feldman Public Relations LA - Public Relations

For international rights inquiries,
please contact: sk@skybound.com

WWW.SKYBOUND.COM

IMAGE COMICS, INC.
Robert Kirkman - chief operating officer
Erik Larsen - chief financial officer
Todd McFarlane - president.
Marc Silvestri - chief executive officer
Jim Valentino - vice-president
Eric Stephenson - publisher
Todd Martinez - sales & licensing coordinator
Sarah deLaine - pr & marketing coordinator
Branwyn Bigglestone - accounts manager
Emily Miller - administrative assistant
Jamie Parreno - marketing assistant
Kevin Yuen - digital rights coordinator
Tyler Shainline - production manager
Drew Gill - art director
Jonathan Chan - senior production artist
Monica Garcia - production artist
Vincent Kukua - production artist
Jana Cook - production artist
www.imagecomics.com

THE WALKING DEAD, VOL. 15: WE FIND OURSELVES. First Printing. Published by Image Comics, Inc. Office of publication: 2134 Allston Way, 2nd Floor, Berkeley, California 94704. Copyright © 2011 Robert Kirkman, LLC. All rights reserved. Originally published in single magazine format as THE WALKING DEAD #85-90. THE WALKING DEAD™ (including all prominent characters featured in this issue), its logo and all character likenesses are trademarks of Robert Kirkman, LLC, unless otherwise noted. Image Comics® and its logos are registered trademarks and copyrights of Image Comics, Inc. All rights reserved. No part of this publication may be reproduced or transmitted, in any form or by any means (except for short excerpts for review purposes) without the express written permission of Image Comics, Inc. All names, characters, events and locales in this publication are entirely fictional. Any resemblance to actual persons (living and/or dead), events or places, without satiric intent, is coincidental.

PRINTED IN THE USA. For information regarding the CPSIA on this printed material call:
203-595-3636 and provide reference # EAST – 413856

ISBN: 978-1-60706-440-4

IT'S BEEN NEARLY TWENTY-FOUR HOURS, RICK.

PLEASE, EAT *SOMETHING.*

NOT HUNGRY.

I NEED TO GET BACK OUT THERE. SORRY.

NONSENSE, GLENN. IT'LL BE DARK SOON. THEY'RE ALREADY STARTING TO QUIT. YOU CAN JUST STAY PUT.

OKAY, YOU TWISTED MY ARM.

I'M SO GLAD YOU'RE BACK HERE... I WAS SO WORRIED AND I--

OH, GOD.

MAGGIE, WHAT'S WRONG?

IT'S NOTHING, JUST...

AFTER EVERYTHING I'VE BEEN THROUGH... ALL THE BAD THAT'S HAPPENED. I ACTUALLY FEEL *LUCKY* RIGHT NOW... I'M *HAPPY*...

...AND THAT FEELS SO *WRONG*, WITH EVERYONE WHO DIED...

SURVIVOR'S GUILT... TRUST ME, I'VE HAD IT. IT'S ONLY NATURAL TO FEEL GUILTY FOR BEING HAPPY.

BUT... I FEEL THE EXACT SAME WAY. I LOVE YOU, MAGGIE.

EVERYONE SEEMS ON BOARD WITH MY PLANS. I THINK WE'RE GOING TO BE ABLE TO MAKE THIS WORK.

IT'S HARD... BEING OPTIMISTIC WITH YOU HERE... LIKE THIS.

I'M DOING IT FOR YOU, CARL. I'M TRYING TO THINK OF YOUR FUTURE AND...

WHY AM I DOING THIS? YOU CAN'T HEAR ME.

YOU'RE PROBABLY--

RICK?

WHAT DO YOU MEAN, *MOVED?*

HE LIFTED HIS HEAD, COUGHED.

WHAT DOES IT MEAN?!

COULD MEAN ANYTHING, COULD MEAN NOTHING. COULD YOU... LEAVE FOR A MOMENT?

I'M SORRY, I JUST WANT TO CHECK OUT A FEW THINGS, BEST IF I'M NOT DISTRACTED.

PLEASE.

RICK...

I'M FINE.

RICK?

RICK, IT'S LATE AND... THERE'S NOTHING YOU CAN DO HERE--NO REASON FOR YOU TO BE HERE. PLEASE, IF HE WAKES UP I'LL COME GET YOU MYSELF.

JUST GO HOME AND GET SOME SLEEP. THIS ISN'T GOOD FOR YOU.

IF IT'S ALL THE SAME TO YOU, I'D REALLY LIKE TO STAY AND--

EVERYTHING OKAY?

I'M SORRY, I DIDN'T KNOW...

I'LL... GET OUT OF YOUR HAIR.

HEY.

OH, SORRY.

I DON'T REALLY THINK ABOUT THE PAST... IT'S TOO PAINFUL.

WELL, YOU KNOW... MY GOD... THE THINGS WE'VE ENDURED.

YEAH. YOU CAN GET CAUGHT UP IN DWELLING ON ALL THE HORRIBLE THINGS THAT HAVE HAPPENED...

...IT CAN SLOW YOU DOWN, GET YOU KILLED.

EXACTLY. SO I JUST DON'T DO IT... I RARELY STOP AND REFLECT ON ANYTHING THAT'S HAPPENED.

DOESN'T MEAN I DON'T MISS LORI, I DO--I JUST CAN'T... THINK ABOUT HER TOO MUCH OR IT'S...

IT'S OKAY.

I GET IT.

IT'S JUST, I'M SO ACCUSTOMED TO LIVING IN THE MOMENT, DAY BY DAY, NOT LOOKING AHEAD, NOT LOOKING BACK...

I WAS BLIND TO HOW DIFFICULT THAT MAKES LIFE.

THANKS FOR THIS. REALLY.

IT'S REALLY NOTHING.

CAN'T YOU TASTE IT?

IS THIS BEEF JERKY?

IT'S...

...GOOD.

RICK, DO YOU HAVE A MINUTE?

SURE THING...

MAGGIE.

SOPHIA.

AFTERNOON. NOT MUCH OF A SELECTION IN HERE, OLIVIA.

YEAH. THAT'S ACTUALLY WHAT I WANTED TO TALK TO YOU ABOUT, RICK.

WE'RE STARTING TO RUN PRETTY LOW...

HOW LOW?

WE COULD START TIGHTENING RATIONS, ALTHOUGH I DON'T THINK THAT WOULD GO WELL WITH ALL THIS WORK BEING DONE.

WINTER'S JUST GETTING STARTED... THINGS COULD GET PRETTY BAD HERE IN A FEW WEEKS... AND WE'D BE ALMOST OUT OF FOOD ABOUT THEN.

I THINK WE NEED TO SEND A TEAM OUT, SHORE US UP FOR THE WINTER.

YOU KNOW WHAT SUCKS...

...THE PHONES AREN'T WORKING. IT'S THE LITTLE THINGS, REALLY, THAT I MISS THE MOST.

SPENCER?!

IF THE PHONES WERE WORKING, I'D HAVE JUST CALLED WHEN WE FINISHED DIGGING OUR HOLES.

INSTEAD, I COME OVER TO TALK, UNANNOUNCED BECAUSE... HOW DO YOU ANNOUNCE YOURSELF NOW ANYWAY?

AND THEN I SEE YOU'RE NOT HERE... RATHER THAN GO LOOKING FOR YOU, WHICH SEEMS CREEPY AND WEIRD... I DECIDE TO WAIT FOR YOU HERE.

BUT THEN I FALL ASLEEP WHILE I'M WAITING... AND HERE I AM, HOURS AFTER DARK, BY THE LOOKS OF IT... ON YOUR PORCH...

...BEING CREEPY.

IF ONLY THE PHONES WORKED.

OH...

HOW DID SHE DIE?

SHE WAS CARRYING JUDY... THEY WERE BOTH SHOT.

WHO'S JUDY?

SHE WAS YOUR SISTER...

...SHE WAS...

...JUST A BABY...

STALE POTATO CHIPS-- SCORE!

ANYTHING?

NOTHING.

RICK?

ARE YOU OKAY?

YEAH, IT'S NOTHING.

JUST A LITTLE... WELL... I'M CLEARLY UPSET.

SORRY.

ALL YOU'VE DONE FOR ME? NOT MUCH NEED TO APOLOGIZE FOR ANYTHING.

EVERYONE LOOKS TO ME FOR LEADERSHIP... I'M SUPPOSED TO BE THE STRONG ONE.

I HATE FOR ANYONE TO SEE ME LIKE THIS.

ALL THIS TIME, WHAT WE'VE BEEN THROUGH, TOGETHER... IT'S OKAY.

OKAY?

ANYTHING I CAN DO TO HELP?

NO, IT'S NOTHING.

MY DAD ALWAYS GAVE ME THE WHOLE "BOYS DON'T CRY" SPEECH. I TRIED ALL I COULD TO ADHERE TO THAT... JUST NEVER REALLY WORKED OUT THAT WAY.

FEEL LIKE I'VE ALWAYS BEEN A FEW THOUGHTS FROM CRYING... ALL MY LIFE. MORE SO NOW, WITH EVERYTHING...

NOW THIS LITTLE FUCKER INSIDE IS GOING TO TELL RICK WE'RE ONTO HIM. WE NEED TO TAKE HIM OUT BEFORE RICK RETURNS!

NOT LIKE THIS, MAN.

YOU BETTER MAN UP AND BACK MY PLAY HERE! THIS IS YOUR FATHER'S *LEGACY* AT STAKE.

THIS IS NO TIME FOR COLD GODDAMN FEET.

GLENN! GET OUT HERE BEFORE I COME IN THERE AND KIL EVERY DAMN ONE OF YOU INSIDE!

PUT THE GUN DOWN *NOW!*

GET BACK!

EVERYONE, STAY BACK! IF YOU'RE NOT WITH ME, YOU'RE WITH *THEM!*

WHAT'S THE SAYING... OH, YEAH... "UNITED WE STAND, DIVIDED WE FALL," RIGHT? IT WAS ON THE BACK OF THE *DOLLAR,* FOR CHRIST'S SAKE.

OF COURSE-- IT'S BEEN A WHILE SINCE I LOOKED.

SO, DO I HAVE TO *SAY* ANYTHING ELSE? CAN I JUST LEAVE IT AT THAT? BECAUSE I'M TIRED AND I HAVE *MUCH* BETTER THINGS TO DO.

YOU'RE NOT...

...GOING TO *KILL* US?

YOU THINK WE *WANT* TO KILL YOU?

YOU'RE *STUPIDER* THAN I THOUGHT.

OKAY, THEN. I'LL LEAVE YOU TO BE WITH YOUR SON.

ALL RIGHT. GOOD NIGHT, THEN.

WHAT WAS *THAT* ALL ABOUT?

CHRIST...

WHAT?

I DON'T EVEN KNOW WHERE TO BEGIN...

...THIS WAS ALL *ONE* DAY?

TO BE CONTINUED...

MORE GREAT BOOKS FROM ROBERT KIRKMAN & IMAGE COMICS!

THE ASTOUNDING WOLF-MAN
VOL. 1 TP
ISBN: 978-1-58240-862-0
$14.99
VOL. 2 TP
ISBN: 978-1-60706-007-9
$14.99
VOL. 3 TP
ISBN: 978-1-60706-111-3
$16.99
VOL. 4 TP
ISBN: 978-1-60706-249-3
$16.99

BATTLE POPE
VOL. 1: GENESIS TP
ISBN: 978-1-58240-572-8
$14.99
VOL. 2: MAYHEM TP
ISBN: 978-1-58240-529-2
$12.99
VOL. 3: PILLOW TALK TP
ISBN: 978-1-58240-677-0
$12.99
VOL. 4: WRATH OF GOD TP
ISBN: 978-1-58240-751-7
$9.99

BRIT
VOL. 1: OLD SOLDIER TP
ISBN: 978-1-58240-678-7
$14.99
VOL. 2: AWOL
ISBN: 978-1-58240-864-4
$14.99
VOL. 3: FUBAR
ISBN: 978-1-60706-061-1
$16.99

CAPES
VOL. 1: PUNCHING THE CLOCK TP
ISBN: 978-1-58240-756-2
$17.99

HAUNT
VOL. 1 TP
ISBN: 978-1-60706-154-0
$9.99
VOL. 2 TP
ISBN: 978-1-60706-229-5
$16.99

INVINCIBLE
VOL. 1: FAMILY MATTERS TP
ISBN: 978-1-58240-711-1
$12.99
VOL. 2: EIGHT IS ENOUGH TP
ISBN: 978-1-58240-347-2
$12.99
VOL. 3: PERFECT STRANGERS TP
ISBN: 978-1-58240-793-7
$12.99
VOL. 4: HEAD OF THE CLASS TP
ISBN: 978-1-58240-440-2
$14.95
VOL. 5: THE FACTS OF LIFE TP
ISBN: 978-1-58240-554-4
$14.99
VOL. 6: A DIFFERENT WORLD TP
ISBN: 978-1-58240-579-7
$14.99
VOL. 7: THREE'S COMPANY TP
ISBN: 978-1-58240-656-5
$14.99
VOL. 8: MY FAVORITE MARTIAN TP
ISBN: 978-1-58240-683-1
$14.99
VOL. 9: OUT OF THIS WORLD TP
ISBN: 978-1-58240-827-9
$14.99
VOL. 10: WHO'S THE BOSS TP
ISBN: 978-1-60706-013-0
$16.99
VOL. 11: HAPPY DAYS TP
ISBN: 978-1-60706-062-8
$16.99
VOL. 12: STILL STANDING TP
ISBN: 978-1-60706-166-3
$16.99
VOL. 13: GROWING PAINS TP
ISBN: 978-1-60706-251-6
$16.99
VOL. 14: THE VILTRUMITE WAR TP
ISBN: 978-1-60706-367-4
$19.99
ULTIMATE COLLECTION, VOL. 1 HC
ISBN 978-1-58240-500-1
$34.95
ULTIMATE COLLECTION, VOL. 2 HC
ISBN: 978-1-58240-594-0
$34.99
ULTIMATE COLLECTION, VOL. 3 HC
ISBN: 978-1-58240-763-0
$34.99
ULTIMATE COLLECTION, VOL. 4 HC
ISBN: 978-1-58240-989-4
$34.99
ULTIMATE COLLECTION, VOL. 5 HC
ISBN: 978-1-60706-116-8
$34.99
ULTIMATE COLLECTION, VOL. 6 HC
ISBN: 978-1-60706-360-5
$34.99
THE OFFICIAL HANDBOOK OF THE INVINCIBLE UNIVERSE TP
ISBN: 978-1-58240-831-6
$12.99
INVINCIBLE PRESENTS, VOL. 1: ATOM EVE & REX SPLODE TP
ISBN: 978-1-60706-255-4
$14.99
THE COMPLETE INVINCIBLE LIBRARY, VOL. 2 HC
ISBN: 978-1-60706-112-0
$125.00

THE COMPLETE INVINCIBLE LIBRARY, VOL. 3 HC
ISBN: 978-1-60706-421-3
$125.00
INVINCIBLE COMPENDIUM VOL. 1
ISBN: 978-1-60706-411-4
$64.99

THE WALKING DEAD
VOL. 1: DAYS GONE BYE TP
ISBN: 978-1-58240-672-5
$9.99
VOL. 2: MILES BEHIND US TP
ISBN: 978-1-58240-775-3
$14.99
VOL. 3: SAFETY BEHIND BARS TP
ISBN: 978-1-58240-805-7
$14.99
VOL. 4: THE HEART'S DESIRE TP
ISBN: 978-1-58240-530-8
$14.99
VOL. 5: THE BEST DEFENSE TP
ISBN: 978-1-58240-612-1
$14.99
VOL. 6: THIS SORROWFUL LIFE TP
ISBN: 978-1-58240-684-8
$14.99
VOL. 7: THE CALM BEFORE TP
ISBN: 978-1-58240-828-6
$14.99
VOL. 8: MADE TO SUFFER TP
ISBN: 978-1-58240-883-5
$14.99
VOL. 9: HERE WE REMAIN TP
ISBN: 978-1-60706-022-2
$14.99
VOL. 10: WHAT WE BECOME TP
ISBN: 978-1-60706-075-8
$14.99
VOL. 11: FEAR THE HUNTERS TP
ISBN: 978-1-60706-181-6
$14.99
VOL. 12: LIFE AMONG THEM TP
ISBN: 978-1-60706-254-7
$14.99
VOL. 13: TOO FAR GONE TP
ISBN: 978-1-60706-329-2
$14.99
VOL. 14: NO WAY OUT TP
ISBN: 978-1-60706-392-6
$14.99
VOL. 15: WE FIND OURSELVES TP
ISBN: 978-1-60706-392-6
$14.99
BOOK ONE HC
ISBN: 978-1-58240-619-0
$34.99
BOOK TWO HC
ISBN: 978-1-58240-698-5
$34.99
BOOK THREE HC
ISBN: 978-1-58240-825-5
$34.99

BOOK FOUR HC
ISBN: 978-1-60706-000-0
$34.99
BOOK FIVE HC
ISBN: 978-1-60706-171-7
$34.99
BOOK SIX HC
ISBN: 978-1-60706-327-8
$34.99
BOOK SEVEN HC
ISBN: 978-1-60706-439-8
$34.99
DELUXE HARDCOVER, VOL. 1
ISBN: 978-1-58240-619-0
$100.00
DELUXE HARDCOVER, VOL. 2
ISBN: 978-1-60706-029-7
$100.00
DELUXE HARDCOVER, VOL. 3
ISBN: 978-1-60706-330-8
$100.00
THE WALKING DEAD: THE COVERS, VOL. 1 HC
ISBN: 978-1-60706-002-4
$24.99
THE WALKING DEAD SURVIVORS' GUIDE
ISBN: 978-1-60706-458-9
$12.99

REAPER
GRAPHIC NOVEL
ISBN: 978-1-58240-354-2
$6.95

SUPER DINOSAUR
VOL. 1
ISBN: 978-1-60706-420-6
$9.99
DELUXE COLORING BOOK
ISBN: 978-1-60706-481-7
$4.99

SUPERPATRIOT
AMERICA'S FIGHTING FORCE
ISBN: 978-1-58240-355-1
$14.99

TALES OF THE REALM
HARDCOVER
ISBN: 978-1-58240-426-0
$34.95
TRADE PAPERBACK
ISBN: 978-1-58240-394-6
$14.95

TECH JACKET
VOL. 1: THE BOY FROM EARTH TP
ISBN: 978-1-58240-771-5
$14.99

TO FIND YOUR NEAREST COMIC BOOK STORE, CALL: 1-888-COMIC-BOOK

THE WALKING DEAD™, BRIT™ & CAPES™ © 2011 Robert Kirkman. INVINCIBLE ™ © 2011 Robert Kirkman and Cory Walker. BATTLE POPE ™ © 2011 Robert Kirkman and Tony Moore.
SUPER DINOSAUR & THE ASTOUNDING WOLF-MAN™ © 2011 Robert Kirkman and Jason Howard. TECH JACKET & CLOUDFALL™ © 2011 Robert Kirkman and E.J. Su. REAPER™ and © 2011 Cliff Rathburn.
TALES OF THE REALM™ MVCreations, LLC. © 2011 Matt Tyree & Val Staples. HAUNT™ and © 2011 Todd McFarlane. SUPERPATRIOT™ and © 2011 Erik Larsen. Image Comics® and its logos are registered trademarks of Image Comics, Inc. All rights reserved.